The Child's World of
RESPONSIBILITY

Library of Congress Cataloging-in-Publication Data
Pemberton, N. (Nancy), 1946-
The Child's World of Responsibility/by Nancy Pemberton and Janet
Riehecky. --[Rev.]
p.   cm.
Rev. ed. of: Responsibility. c1988.
Summary: Suggests ways to show responsibility, such as remembering
to feed the cat, putting candy wrappers in the trash can, and going to
bed without fussing.
ISBN 1-56766-392-3 (alk. paper)
1. Responsibility—Juvenile literature. [1. Responsibility.
2. Behavior.] I. Riehecky, Janet, 1953- . II. Pemberton, N. (Nancy).
1946- Responsibility. III. Title.
BJ1451.P46 1997
170'.83--dc21   96-39559
                                           CIP
                                           AC

The Child's World of
RESPONSIBILITY

By N. Pemberton and J. Riehecky • Illustrated by Mechelle Ann

THE CHILD'S WORLD®

What is responsibility?

Responsibility is remembering to give your kitten food and water every day.

Responsibility is hanging up your coat when you come home.

Putting candy wrappers in the trash can, not on the ground, shows responsibility.

Admitting you broke your grandma's china doll—and not blaming your little sister—shows responsibility.

When the baby-sitter doesn't know how many cookies you're allowed, responsibility is taking only the two Mom said you could have.

16

Showing responsibility is going to bed without fussing when the baby-sitter says it's time.

Looking out for a younger child is responsibility. You can hold his hand and remind him to look both ways before crossing the street.

Responsibility is thinking of others, not just of yourself. And it's doing what you're supposed to do, when you're supposed to do it.

Can you think of other ways to show responsibility?